Busy day

Catherine and Laurence Anholt

Hanging washing in the sun.

Fold the clothes for everyone.

Wash the dishes, rub, rub, rub.

Clean the car, scrub, scrub, scrub.

Soon my bedroom will be pink.

Don't cry, baby! Here's your drink.

Pick some flowers in a bunch.

Make some cakes for after lunch.

Growing plants in tidy rows.

Feed the baby, wipe his nose.

Choosing apples for our tea.

I can help you find the key.

Sweeping on an autumn day.

Help me put my toys away.

Is there time for one last play?